Freddy the Frog Finds a Friendly Family

Book 1

Written by Carol Gravante

Illustrated by Kaelen Felix

Edited by Deborah A. Hoffman PhD

All my love, xoxo
- Kaelen E. Felix

This book is based on a true event from Elinor's adventures.
The character names, places and incidents are a figment of the author's imagination.

© Copyright EL4Kids Corp 2019

All rights reserved. No part of this book may be reproduced or used in any commerical manner without a written permission of the copyright owner (EL4Kids) except for fair use of quotation marks in a book review. To order additional copies of this book series contact EL4kids.org.

First U.S. Edition 2019

Written by Carol Gravante
Book Design and Illustrations by Kaelen Felix
Edited by Deborah A. Hoffman, PhD

ISBN: 9781676405580
Imprint: Independently published

The illustrations were traditionally created in watercolor, goauche, ink and colored pencils.

Subscribe to EL4kids non-profit newsletter and join Freddy the Foster Frog's Facebook Fan Page.

Dedicated to all the children in foster care and to those waiting for a forever family.

--C.G. and EL

James 1:27

"Religion that God our Father accepts as pure and faultless is this:

To look after orphans and widows in their distress and to keep oneself from being polluted by the world."

Carol and Elinor want to acknowledge and thank, above all, God for trusting us with this story. Thank you especially to Kim with Millard & Lillian Prutky's Trust for her advocacy of our new sons and for the great start-up help with this effort! It would have been very difficult to get this off the ground without her donation!

Thanks to Carol's husband, Joe, and all of their sons, their extended family, Donna Maddox-Dunn, Alina Sewell, the Nazario family, and the many who gave their input as they are appreciated for their patience and prayer support for these past three years creating the story.

Last, but not least, Kaelen Felix, whose superior illustrations create whimsy, drama, and fun! This story wouldn't be as effective without her willingness to see this through with such creative genius.

More acknowledgements are on WWW.EL4KIDS.ORG

Table of Contents

Introduction   1

Chapter 1   Elinor Finds Freddy   2

Chapter 2   Freddy's Sad Story   6

Chapter 3   Elinor and Freddy Relax at Home   14

Chapter 4   Friends Find Fun   20

Chapter 5   Freddy and Friends Have Fun Helping   28

Chapter 6   Fun Way Up High   36

Introduction

This fabled story with a twist of rhyme is something you'll not often find.

Animals and rhymes are used to create a very safe place to explore deep emotions and seek God's grace.

To safely look through a troubled past,
we highly suggest you not go very fast.
The slower you go and the deeper you dig,
those hurting splinters are big like a twig.

It's much easier with animals and rhyme
to recall painful memories
one at a time.

This is a fabled story about Freddy, the frog with a troubled life and how kind, old Elinor saved him from further strife.

While reading this story,
you might find yourself wandering
down your own rabbit trail…
So, let the story lead you so God's plan can prevail.
As memories arise, you can heal from the past
and become free from pain
that doesn't have to last.

Chapter 1
Elinor Finds Freddy

One evening many, many months ago
        after watching her favorite variety
            show

Elinor found a little frog hiding
outside behind the trash.

Sadly, she noticed that his eye
had a large gash.

Frightened little Freddy
looked very mad.

He was loudly wailing
and was more than sad.

Even though they loved him,
he no longer lived with his
mom and dad.

Elinor had seen children alone
before but had never adopted one
found right outside her door.

Like most frogs...

Freddy liked to jump from log to log,
    hopping around in the thick, cold fog.

      He ate lots of crunchy, wiggly bugs
        with all his friends, the slippery slugs.

          To some, frogs are speckled and mostly charming,
            but to others they're creepy and awfully alarming.

          Tagpoles hatch out of eggs with their sisters and brothers,
            and might hang out with their fathers and mothers.

They also go to frog school
to learn and play,

and most of them
have many
fun days.

But unlike most frogs…

Freddy's family who lived in the shack by the pond,
kept him from roaming a way on beyond.

The one night he left, hoping no one would see;
He hopped and he ran, as frightened as could be.

Exhausted he fell, but went on with no plan,
until he went tripping and limping to hide
by the trash can.

Elinor had a very young and loving heart
and though now old, she longed to do her part.

Even at the age of ninety-three,
she still felt as if she was nineteen.
Fearless and full of life,
she didn't want to miss a thing.

Elinor's heart grew big overtime
and knew that not helping
would have been a crime.

Not all stories end in adoption,
but eventually this story does.

So, when old Elinor finally adopted Freddy,
the news was all a buzz.

Chapter 2
Freddy's Sad Story

So, why tell the end of the story right from the start?
Some of this tale won't be for the faint of heart.

There are some sad parts and scary parts too.
Also, there are fun and laughs as Freddy grew.

So, after raising her own children the best she knew how,
Elinor found herself alone without a pal.

"Now what will I do with my very long days?"
she sighed as she shuffled slowly down the hallway.

"How do I help others in desperate need?
At this phase in life, I can help orphans succeed."
Elinor believed adoption satisfied her desire.
Then realized it wasn't all about her.
Her purpose was higher.

So, when Elinor found Freddy hiding behind the trash one night,
she thought this might be another chance
to do what's right.

She found Freddy rubbing his eye and moaning,
as he sighed and loudly cried.

This seemed really hard for a tough little guy.

"Why are you here? Is your eye hurting?"

Elinor begged him to explain.

"Are you lame? Is your ankle badly sprained?"

Elinor finally realized that her questions were rude.
She didn't even know this cute, little dude

Looking up
to see wrinkles
 and a very
  big smile,

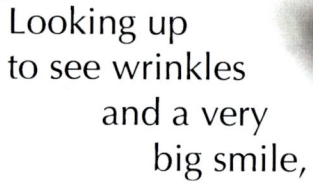

Freddy thought no one
had cared for him
in a while.

Freddy was afraid to tell her
 why he was hiding.

To talk or not to talk,
 he had trouble deciding.

He naturally felt guilty and a little ashamed and wrongfully
 thought he was to blame.

Freddy desperately tried to explain as he started to cry.
 "I told my teacher what happened to my eye.
  My dad said to tell the officers I fell over a pail.
   But they didn't believe him, and so they took him to jail."

Freddy continued with his terrible tale.
 "Then my mom became sick and very frail.
  She couldn't get out of bed and lost her job."
   He was trying very hard not to sob.

Freddy told Elinor that his family
couldn't take care of him anymore.

"I was left alone most of the time, and we were very poor.
We couldn't live in the house any longer rent free,
and the owners of the house, they took the key."

Then he loudly groaned,
"Today the ambulance finally came for my mom,
and I'm now all alone."

He was so scared of the ambulance driver
that he stayed behind the trash.
Reliving this caused his mind to thrash.

With eyes wildly looking this way and that,
he flopped on the wet ground with an unfortunate splat!

"No one will want me," he cried...his emotions to convey...

"It's been a very bad, horrible day!"

Though Freddy was spilling his guts to someone he didn't know,
somehow it felt safe for his emotions to show.

Elinor softly dried his tears, whispering,
"I'm so sorry…Would you like to go with me inside
so I can try to fix your eye?"

She told him that she had adopted many children in need
and helped them know Love and how to succeed.

With a twinkle in his good eye,
Freddy looked up and grinned.
His heart began to flutter
from deep within.

"Can I stay with you for a while?"
he said, with new hope and a
shy little smile.

Putting her finger under
his slimy green chin,
"My, my you're mighty thin.
Yes, of course. I'll take you in."

Freddy's new life was about to begin...

Chapter 3
Elinor and Freddy Relax at Home

Elinor's house was nestled between water and trees.

It was not cluttered and scrubbed nice and clean.
Freddy felt as if he were in a perfect dream.

As he sat in the window finally at ease,
Freddy could hear the gentle breeze.

Musical sounds of other frogs were chirping.
Instantly the memories of the past were lurking.

Taken far back and now fully spellbound,
his lonely heart said, "Pitter pat…pound."

Freddy missed his froggy friends at the quarry
still living outside in their natural territory.

But he realized he was living in an awesome place with
possible new friends in his own special space.

In his new house, he smelled a hint from his past.
The aroma of Elinor's perfume made him downcast.

The scent took him far back to the safe place
with his Grandma's embrace and her sweet face.

He began to sweat and fully fret with her memory
he hadn't dealt with yet...

Freddy often talked in group therapy,
about his many feelings, and the group had to agree.

They all worked hard to deal with their past
so those painful emotions would heal and not last.

Rex

Sue

Freddy

Junior

Yankee

Elinor was nice, and Freddy realized she would standby.
Coming to his rescue and drying his good eye,
she quickly became his best ally.

She comforted him,
"You'll meet new friends with arms open wide…
Friends that will surely stick by your side."

Freddy was welcomed by her family
who became his new friends.

However, he wanted his old friendships to never end.
He felt he had deserted them and that was hard to defend.

But then Elinor's shepherd, Yankee,
told him all about the family tree.

He met Rex, the red hound dog, and little Junior the baby frog.
Junior looked like his twin.
Freddy felt glad he fit right in.

Sue, a beautiful brown owl,
offered him a welcome gift
of a personalized hand towel.

The love Sue poured on Freddy
made him feel adored.

With life in this new house,
he was never bored.

He learned that like him,
Elinor's family had struggled in much the same way,
and their acceptance of him saved the day.

But it was Yankee who soon became
Freddy's very best buddy,
offering to assist with his classes
and help him study.

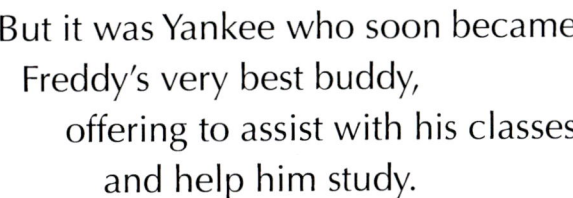

When Yankee smiled at him with a big toothy grin,
Freddy felt better about himself and less of a has-been.

Chapter 4
Friends Find Fun

Sue with her amazing eyesight and hearing that was first rate,
was a brand new buddy…a fun playmate.

She hooted and screeched full of glee
from a height that only she could sightsee.

"Sue, come right down out of the tree
and play this awesome game with me!"

Rex organized all the races in the back street,
and there was rarely a time when he experienced defeat.

He redirected his anger and learned to run…
finding a healthy outlet but now didn't want to be outdone.

Learning how to gracefully win and lose well
was something Elinor taught him so his pride wouldn't swell.

Rex had trouble with this in his past
   but now encouraging others was what she had asked.

He began to see true wisdom because it was all
   about Love, straight from his new perfect
   Father up above.

Then Junior showed his skills with a jump and a hop,
   leaping over the river rocks, landing right on top.

He also learned about being a good sport,
   putting others first, and their achievements report.

The family quickly grew to love Freddy's fun side, too.

He loved to run and hide
   and then jump out, hollering

"Boo!"

"APPLE, PEACHES, PUMPKIN PIE,
   WHO'S NOT READY, HOLLER, 'AYE'"

"READY OR NOT! HERE I COME!"

They were always ready for family fun.

A new neighbor, a spiky and cute hedgehog named Finn,
showed up to play, his clothes held by a pin.

Finn

Life at home for him was rather grim,
as he was often left alone, and he'd lost his grin.

Elinor sensed there was more to his story,
and felt he needed love and not to be discriminatory.

He'd come to play hide-and-seek till the day was done,
as time spent at Elinor's was a lot more fun.

But during play others would search for what seemed like hours,
often forgetting he liked hiding in the garden flowers.

He would go very, very deep underground
and would stay quiet, barely making a sound
until they begged for him to be found.

**COME OUT! COME OUT, WHEREVER YOU ARE!
YOU'VE TAKEN THIS THING, WAY TOO FAR!"**

Elinor taught them to play hopscotch and other games too.

Their crazy antics made the house fun like a zoo.

They all had their own unique language and traditions,
which might have made it hard
with their unusual conditions.

Snuffles and **squeals** was the language that Finn spoke.

Freddy and Junior would **grunt, chirp, ribbit** and **croak.**

Yankee and Rex would often **howl** or **bark,**
especially when chasing a squirrel at the park.

Sue, the owl, would often **hoot** and **screech,**
and everyone had very different **speech.**

Their differences might have made it incredibly hard,
but it didn't really matter when they played in the yard.

Late in the afternoon, Elinor called,
"Dinner is ready so come wash your faces."

They were never ready to come in from the races,
but they knew to be polite and respect Elinor's place.

They loved her old table set with linen and lace.

Elinor taught them that true families together should play,
and eat together...every single day.

Bowing their heads to give thanks was new,
And at first they thought praying was a bunch of hullabaloo,

But over time, they realized the secret of saying grace.

Giving thanks in all things?

They learned gratitude had its place!

LOVE	COURAGE
ACCEPTANCE	JOY
MERCY	PEACE
HOPEFULNESS	PATIENCE
COMPASSION	KINDNESS
EMPATHY	GENTLENESS
HELPFULNESS	GOODNESS
FAITHFULNESS	SELF-CONTROL
HUMBLENESS	GENEROSITY

Chapter 5
Freddy and Friends Have Fun Helping

𝓕reddy and Elinor got along just fine,
and it only took a little bit of time
to see that Elinor needed a lot of help.
Once she fell down and let out a YELP.

She often cleaned until she was dizzy.
Working many hours, she was always so busy.

Although Elinor was active, she was very old.
Working while using her walker was a sight to behold.

She would have to cook breakfast and all other meals
because she knew this was part of the deal...
helping her children grow, and with
God's help to heal.

No matter how hard Elinor worked,
there were still dust bunnies that secretly lurked
under the beds and in the hall...
the children tracked in dirt while bouncing their ball.

Muddy footprints and lots of sticky slime
kept her busy with mopping up the grime.

Washing the windows during spring cleaning,
was very hard 'cause the ladder was leaning.

It was way too high for her to climb.
She better not fall! That would be a crime!

Learning that life was not all about him,
Freddy decided to act on a whim.

He jumped up to clean the windows until they shined.
Eventually, to lighten her load became a favorite pastime.

The others noticed Freddy helping to clean.
They knew that by not helping, they were all being mean.

So, they all pitched in happily now to help their mother,
because finishing the chores was actually helping each other.

Now they all knew that they'd have fun
when the housework was finally done.

Sue, with her amazing eyesight
was best at finding the dirt.

Yankee, the German shepherd, dusted with his shirt,
using dusting polish with just a little squirt.

Rex, the hound dog, raced around
and mopped with his tail,
accidently tripping over the very full pail.

Rex, filled with dread, hid behind the couch…
trying to disappear in a desperate crouch.

Elinor didn't get angry 'cause she knew they were unskilled.
but, Junior thought it was funny that the pail dumped and spilled.

He laughed and giggled as he hopped and spun,
turning any frowns upside down till they were done.

Everyone including Rex smiled…their hearts he had won.

Elinor watched them work without any pay.
Yes, teaching responsibility, Elinor had a lot to say.

She used their home as a learning place, to impart
life concepts and positive character traits.

She took them with her to volunteer
and told hero stories that made them stand up and cheer.

Elinor was tired at night and would rely on prayer.
You see, she did this with God's strength, love and care.

At the end of the day even though she was weary,
she knew to talk to God, and her eyes got teary.

Elinor had a mom that said, "You're a crybaby…so stop!"
She learned not to cry and accept her hard lot.
Much later in life she found out crying was okay,
And knew God caught her tears when she bowed to pray.

The children sang and danced while doing their chores.
   Otherwise, it could have been a terrible bore.

When the work was done, Elinor cooked them all
   their dinners. Talking about how each helped,
      made them all feel like winners.

Then she served pie with frothy whipped cream
   and whispered, "I'm glad we worked together
      as a team to keep the house nice and clean."

Tick Tock...
   It was 8 o'clock and Elinor said it was late
      and time for all to go to sleep, but the
         children wanted to wait.

And Freddy, as usual, was not really ready
   and wouldn't count the sheep.
      Instead, he leaped on the bed
         then fell on the floor in a heap.

Then the others started jumping up and down...
   playing leapfrog as if going across town.

Patient Elinor was used to Freddy jumping like a frog,
   and she knew they'd soon be sleeping like a log.

They were grateful to God for a super family
and thanked Him for keeping them safe from calamity.

Clasping their hands, they bowed their heads in prayer,
their words simple, and without special flair:

Now I lay me down to sleep.
I pray the Lord my soul to keep.

Watch and guide me through the night,
and wake me with the morning light.

Thank you for Elinor 'cause she took us in
and let us become one of her kin.

Chapter 6
Fun Way Up High

There came a day sometime in May
when Elinor directed the children's play.
Fear was now being whittled away.

She knew they'd never had a chance
to zip line across the great expanse
because of their previous circumstance.

But with the idea of going fast on a zip line,
she hoped their courage was now just fine.

Elinor thoughtfully approached timid Freddy,
looking as though he was certainly not ready.

Freddy reluctantly said, "Hmmmm… yeah, okay,
but I would prefer to play lawn croquet."

Don't you want to resolve the lessons from the past
by crossing those cables with us at last?"

"Do you remember the old hymn, "Safe am I,"
by Mildred Leightner Dillon?"

She sang to them as they swayed to the music and echoed her song...

"Safe am I... Safe am I...

In the hollow of His hand.

Sheltered o're... Sheltered o're...

In His love forever more.

No will can harm me, no foe alarm me.

For He keeps both day and night.

Safe am I...Safe am I....

In the hollow of His hand."

Convinced now that God would protect him…

Freddy did his best to go along with the fun,
but then surely said, "I'll be glad when this day is done."

The others knew that Freddy might struggle to be brave
as he'd come partly out of his fear-filled cave.

They had watched him attempt new things that were hard,
but knew in their hearts, now he was rarely off-guard.

Freddy enjoyed the adventures they'd found their way into,
helping him grow with each amazing breakthrough.

Each of them struggled with their own emotional baggage,
but now God's love gave a more even advantage.

And the love and care that their mother bestowed,
   helped them halt a destructive mode.

They didn't want to lose their shine for life
   just because they had experienced awful strife.

The rotten rust from calamity God scrubbed away
   to make room for more hip-hop hoorays!

Sue found it easy to fly amongst the trees.
   "I'm tied in tight between my knees.
    These safety straps make me feel squeezed."

Looking up at the zip line,
   Freddy was finally at ease.

"Let me jump into the harness and zoom away!"
   As he smiled and took off without delay.

Rex offered to help Junior who was now in tears.
   Although Junior had grown in the past years…

And now growing fast by leaps and bounds,
   he still couldn't see himself so high off the ground.

But when Freddy made a choice not to stay on land,
he'd determined to be a role model
and take command.

Junior eventually whispered to Elinor, "This isn't easy!"
As they all zipped away
But saw over and over,
they had returned to play.

"I'd like to try. Maybe it won't seem so high…"
Imagining himself as a butterfly.

Elinor enthusiastically paid his way
and watched Junior face his fear and zip away.

The joy Elinor saw on everyone's faces
   made her feel like she wanted to trade places.

Knowing she was old, yes, more than old,
   she felt she didn't need to be told.

She thought it would be wise to stay on the ground
   and enjoy watching the adventures they had found.

She worried that maybe she shouldn't risk her health.

Had she let doctors put her fun on the shelf?

Yet, at age ninety-three, she still had spunk
   and refused the fear that had put her in a funk.

"In my heart I feel I'm still nineteen,
   and I really don't want to miss a thing."

Elinor chatted with the tour guides
   as they encouraged her to try.

They assured her she'd be safe, high in the sky.

She had to decide, "Should I try and fly?"

Now fitted with straps, the children cheered,
acknowledging her effort as fear disappeared.

She put on the straps, but faith in God held her up.
She soared high above rivers and beautiful buttercups.

Everyone thought she might give out a loud scream,
but not brave Elinor as she realized this dream.

Freddy got her permission to post her fearless flight
on Social Media Livestream without a fight.

She was grateful to God Almighty, up above,
remembering her life of adventure and His endless Love.

More fabled stories to come...

Watch for upcoming adventures where all the characters work through their past memories with the help of God's love.

Catch and Release

This activity helps families to see the good in others. Learning one character trait everyday increases vocabulary and understanding of the positive and negative traits.

This encourages families to model and practice positive character traits as everyone knows they are being watched.

Directions

Catch a "Family Frog" at Breakfast

Watch for Good Character Traits all Day

Reveal Your Frog at the Dinner Table

**Tell Family What You Observed
and What They Did Well**

Watch Family Freedom Flourish!

Make copies one frog per family member

Have fun drawing the story's characters in your own style and post them to <u>info@EL4Kids.Org</u> to be displayed on the website at <u>www.el4kids.org</u>

Selected winners could be shown book #2. Coming soon.

Marissa G.

Gabe

Lydia

ABOUT CAROL AND ELINOR!

Carol met Elinor when she heard a God-thought.
"Stop! She has a story."

Freddy the Foster Frog book series was written under divine inspiration over three years.

It is inspired by Elinor's life and faith journey but also an important event, Carol heard the God thought,

***"Put the frog by the trash can, this is a significant adoption story, start taking pictures.
This will raise money for adoption."***

When Elinor found the frog by the trash...the story unfolded.

Carol took many pictures of Elinor and Freddy and wrote the story based on her and her husband's experience adopting teens while they were in their 60's *Freddy the Foster Frog* is a fabled story with a twist of rhyme.

It's used in all environments as a window, door and mirror to bring empathy, compassion and healing.

Find out more about Carol and Elinor's backstory on:
WWW.EL4KIDS.ORG

ABOUT KAELEN FELIX

Kaelen Felix is an illustrator and graphic designer from Saint Louis, Missouri where she currently resides.

She is a graduate of Memphis College of Art with a Bachelor of Fine Arts (BFA) in Illustration.

She is also member of the **Children's Book Writers and Illustrators** (SCBWI) since 2018.

Her passion for art started around two years of age! Today, she continues to dedicate her freelance time to illustrating and designing children's books.

Freddy The Foster Frog: Finds a Friendly Family is her second illustrated and published book.

Fun fact: Carol and Kaelen met at a choir reunion in Fall 2014 and in the Fall of 2018, and thereafter, began this collaboration inspired by Elinor's story.

Check out her social media accounts below!

@kaelix_fx (instagram) **@kaex_fx** (twitter)

For more information on Kaelen's upcoming publications, visit her website below at:
www.kaelenfelix.com

Carol (Left) with the Illustrator Kaelen Felix (Right)

Made in the USA
Columbia, SC
10 January 2020